A NOTE TO PARENTS

Reading Aloud with Your Child
Research shows that reading books aloud is the single most valuable support parents can provide in helping children learn to read.

- Be a ham! The more enthusiasm you display, the more your child will enjoy the book.
- Run your finger underneath the words as you read to signal that the print carries the story.
- Leave time for examining the illustrations more closely; encourage your child to find things in the pictures.
- Invite your youngster to join in whenever there's a repeated phrase in the text.
- Link up events in the book with similar events in your child's life.
- If your child asks a question, stop and answer it. The book can be a means to learning more about your child's thoughts.

Listening to Your Child Read Aloud
The support of your attention and praise is absolutely crucial to your child's continuing efforts to learn to read.

- If your child is learning to read and asks for a word, give it immediately so that the meaning of the story is not interrupted. DO NOT ask your child to sound out the word.
- On the other hand, if your child initiates the act of sounding out, don't intervene.
- If your child is reading along and makes what is called a miscue, listen for the sense of the miscue. If the word "road" is substituted for the word "street," for instance, no meaning is lost. Don't stop the reading for a correction.
- If the miscue makes no sense (for example, "horse" for "house"), ask your child to reread the sentence because you're not sure you understand what's just been read.
- Above all else, enjoy your child's growing command of print and make sure you give lots of praise. *You are your child's first teacher—and the most important one. Praise from you is critical for further risk-taking and learning.*

— Priscilla Lynch
Ph.D., New York University
Educational Consultant

Text copyright © 1977 by Margaret Parish.
Illustrations copyright © 1977 by Lynn Sweat.
All rights reserved. Published by Scholastic Inc., 555 Broadway,
New York, NY 10012, by arrangement with Greenwillow Books,
a division of William Morrow & Company, Inc.
HELLO READER!, CARTWHEEL BOOKS, and the CARTWHEEL BOOKS
logo are registered trademarks of Scholastic Inc.
The HELLO READER! logo is a trademark of Scholastic Inc.

ISBN 0-590-53773-3

20 19 18 17   8   9/9 0/0

Printed in the U.S.A.   23

TEACH US, AMELIA BEDELIA

by Peggy Parish
Illustrated by Lynn Sweat

Hello Reader! — Level 4

SCHOLASTIC INC.

Cartwheel
·B·O·O·K·S·®

New York Toronto London Auckland Sydney

The telephone was ringing.

"I'm coming, I'm coming,"

said Amelia Bedelia.

She answered the telephone.

"Mrs. Rogers!" she said.

"Where are you?"

5

"I'm at the airport
in Pinewood,"
said Mrs. Rogers.
"You didn't tell me
you were going away,"
said Amelia Bedelia.
"I'm not," said Mrs. Rogers.
"I'm meeting the new teacher.
But her plane is late."
"That's too bad,"
said Amelia Bedelia.

"The telephone at the school
   is out of order,"
   Mrs. Rogers went on.
"Please go to Mr. Carter's office
   at the school. Tell him what I said."
"I'll go right now,"
   said Amelia Bedelia.

Amelia Bedelia got her things.

She walked to school.

"Where is Mr. Carter's office?"

she asked.

"That first door," said a child.

Amelia Bedelia walked in.

"Mrs. Rogers tried to call you,"
she said. "But your telephone
is out of order."
"I know," said Mr. Carter.
"But thank goodness you're here.
The children are going wild.
Miss Lane left a list for today.
I'll take you to the room."
He handed Amelia Bedelia the list.

"Follow me," he said.

They went down the hall.

Mr. Carter opened a door.

Children were all over the place.

"All right," said Mr. Carter.

"Quiet! This is your new teacher."

"Me! Teach!" said Amelia Bedelia.

But Mr. Carter was gone.

She looked at the children.

They looked at her.

"I'm Amelia Bedelia," she said.

The children giggled.

"You're nice," said Amelia Bedelia.

"I do like happy children.

But we have a lot to do."

She held up the list.

"We must do just what this says,"
she said. "Now, what's first?"

Amelia Bedelia read,

" 'Call the roll.' "

She looked puzzled.

"Call the roll! What roll?"

she said.

"Does anybody have a roll?"

"I have," said Peter.

"Do get it," said Amelia Bedelia.

Peter opened his lunch box.

"Here it is," he said.

"Now I have to call it,"
said Amelia Bedelia.
"Roll! Hey, roll!
All right, that takes care of that."
The children roared.

Amelia Bedelia read her list.

"Land sakes," she said.

"Listen to this.

'Sing a song.'

I never was much of a hand

at singing.

But it says sing a song.

So I'll sing."

And she did!

"More! More!" shouted the children.

"No," said Amelia Bedelia.

"It said *a* song. I did just that."

"Ahh," said the children.

"Now it's reading time,"
said Amelia Bedelia.
"I know about that.
I read my cookbook.
It tells me just what to do."
She held up a book.
She said, "Is this the right one?"
"Yes," said Amanda.

Amelia Bedelia opened the book.

"I declare," she said.

"This is a good one.

Are you ready?"

"Yes," said the children.

"All right," said Amelia Bedelia.

"It says, 'Run, run, run.'"

The children just sat.

Amelia Bedelia clapped her hands.

"Run," she said. "Run, run, run."

Amelia Bedelia ran.

The children ran after her.
Around the room,
through the halls,
around the block they ran.

Finally they ran
back into the room.

Amelia Bedelia plopped on her chair.

"That takes care of run, run, run,"
she said.

"Your book plumb tired me out.

Let's see what's next.

I hope we don't have to run

to do it." She looked at the list.

She said, "It's science time.

Each of you should plant a bulb.

Do you know about that?"

"Yes," said Tim.

"We brought our pots."

"Where are the bulbs?"
said Amelia Bedelia.

"In the top closet," said Rebecca.

"Miss Lane said so."

Amelia Bedelia looked and looked.

"Nothing here but some
dried-up onions," she said.

"You all go outside.

Put some soil in your pots.

I'll go buy some bulbs."

Amelia Bedelia went to the store.

She hurried back.

The children were waiting.

"Here's a bulb for you and you,"

said Amelia Bedelia.

She gave everybody a bulb.

The children looked surprised.

Then they started giggling.

But they planted those bulbs.

They put the pots on the window sill.

"Those do look right pretty,"
said Amelia Bedelia.

"And I learned something new.
I didn't know you could plant bulbs."

Suddenly a bell rang.

"What's that for?"

said Amelia Bedelia.

"Free time," yelled the children.

"Good," said Amelia Bedelia.

The children ran outside.

Amelia Bedelia sat down to rest.

Then free time ended.

Back came the children.

"It's quiet time now,"

said Amelia Bedelia.

"You're supposed to read stories."

Each child chose a book.

All was quiet.

"Why aren't you reading?"

said Amelia Bedelia.

"We are,"

said Ed.

"I don't hear you," said Amelia Bedelia.

The children looked at Amelia Bedelia.

They looked at each other.

And Amelia Bedelia heard them all right.

"My, I'll be glad when quiet time is over,"

she said. "My ears hurt."

Jeff said, "Art comes next.

That's fun."

Amelia Bedelia looked at her list.

"You're right," she said.

"You must paint pictures now."

The children got sheets of art paper.

"What are you doing?"
said Amelia Bedelia.
"We're going to
paint pictures,"
said Bud.
"But how can you?"
said Amelia Bedelia.
"There's no picture there to paint."
"We'll make pictures," said Mary.
"Oh no!" said Amelia Bedelia.
"This says to paint pictures.
You can't paint a picture
without a picture to paint.

Better find one for yourselves."

The children ran around the room.

Not a picture was left on the wall.

But all the children were painting.

Soon the pictures were back on the wall.

"They sure look different," said Steve.

"Yes," said Amelia Bedelia.

"Mr. Carter will be surprised."

The children shook their heads.

"He sure will," said Janet.

"What's next?" said Jamie.

"Our play," said Rebecca.

"We have to practice our play."

"Practice play!" said Amelia Bedelia.

"You mean children have to practice play?

School sure has changed since I went.

All right, out you go."

"But Amelia Bedelia," said the children.

"No buts," said Amelia Bedelia.

"Let's go. Start playing.

Practice that jumping rope some more,"
said Amelia Bedelia.

"I can do better than that."

"Show us," said Janet.

And Amelia Bedelia did.

"I can run faster than that,"
said Amelia Bedelia.
"Show us," said Steve.
So Amelia Bedelia did.

"That's fine," she said. "You've practiced
long enough. Let's go inside.

Let me see what's next,"

said Amelia Bedelia.

"Here are some problems for you."

"Yuck!" said the children.

"Ginny, get your apples,"

said Amelia Bedelia.

"What apples?" said Ginny.

Amelia Bedelia looked puzzled.

She said, "But it says

Ginny has four apples.

Paul takes away two.

Oops," said Amelia Bedelia.
"I don't think I was
supposed to tell that part."
She read the other problems.
"These all have apples in them,"
she said. "Does anybody have apples?"
The children shook their heads.

Then Amelia Bedelia had an idea.

"Let's go to my house," she said.

"We have lots of apples."

"Yes!" shouted the children.

"We better leave a note,"
said Amelia Bedelia.
She went to the blackboard
and wrote,

Then off they went
to the Rogers' backyard.

Amelia Bedelia got the apples.

She called some children.

"There is a problem
for each of you," she said.

"You all have apples.
Somebody is going to try
to take some away.
Are you going to let them?"

"No!" shouted the children.

Amelia Bedelia went
to the other children.
"You are supposed to take away
some of their apples," she said.
She told each child
whom to take from.
"Can you do that?" she said.
"Sure!" said the children.

"All right, everybody,"
said Amelia Bedelia. "Go!"
Children started after each other.
They ran all over the yard.

Amelia Bedelia turned
and went into the kitchen.
She put some of this and
a lot of that into a big pot.
She put the pot on the stove.
"There," she said.
"I'll surprise them."

Amelia Bedelia started out.

Just then Mr. Rogers started in.

"What is all of this?" said Mr. Rogers.

"What are those children doing?"

"Math," said Amelia Bedelia.

"Math!" said Mr. Rogers.

"Come see," said Amelia Bedelia.

They went out.

"That's not fair, Steve," yelled Janet.

"You hid your apples.

I can't take any."

"That's not fair, Judy," shouted Andy.

"You took away all my apples."

"What in tarnation are they doing?"

said Mr. Rogers.

Amelia Bedelia read

him the problems.

"That sounds like fun.

I'm going to help them," he said.

He joined the children.

"Now that does beat all,"

said Amelia Bedelia.

She went inside.

Later she called,

"Everybody come.

All apples on the table."

Apples came from everywhere.

Amelia Bedelia put a stick in each one.

Then she dipped them in the pot.

"Taffy apples!" everybody shouted.

"Right," said Amelia Bedelia.

"Take one and go home. School is out."

The children grabbed apples.

They crowded around Amelia Bedelia.

"Please, please teach us again,"

each one said.

Amelia Bedelia said nothing.
She looked at her kitchen
and shook her head.
Mrs. Rogers walked in.
Someone was with her.

"What happened?" she said.

"Where are the children?"

"Home," said Amelia Bedelia.

"Home!" said Mrs. Rogers.

"But it's not time."

"It was for me,"
   said Amelia Bedelia.

"This is Miss Reed," said Mrs. Rogers.

"She is the new teacher.

She came to get the children."

"Then she will have to find them,"
said Amelia Bedelia.

"I'm plumb tired out."

"But, but . . ." said Miss Reed.

"More taffy apples," called Mr. Rogers.

"Taffy apples!" said Mrs. Rogers.

"Come on, Miss Reed."

Amelia Bedelia put the taffy apples
on the table.

They all sat down and ate.

"I'll let you teach anytime,"

  said Miss Reed,

"if you will make taffy apples."

"Be glad to," said Amelia Bedelia.

"I do love children."